12 OPHELIAS

(a play with broken songs)

By Caridad Svich

12 OPHELIAS

(a play with broken songs)

By

Caridad Svich

WITHDRAWN

NoPassport Press
Theatre & Performance PlayTexts

NoPassport Press
Theatre & Performance PlayTexts
New edition 2008 by NoPassport Press
PO Box 1786, South Gate, CA 90280 USA; -
NoPassportPress@aol.com

ISBN: 978-0-615-24918-6. US List Price: $12.95

12 OPHELIAS

(a play with broken songs)

CONTENTS

Acknowledgments

This play is a result of my ongoing dialogue with Shakespeare and the language of *Hamlet*. Through text and movement work with director Debbie Saivetz, first at Vassar College hosted by Powerhouse Theater and New York Stage & Film, and later at Red Bull Theater and New Georges in New York City, the play was revealed. Musically, the work of Michael Ray Escamilla and Michael Gladis was crucial. The many actors who have been part of the journey of *12 Ophelias* will always be part of its textual memory. Thanks to Eric Krebs, Baruch Performing Arts Center, Baruch College, John Most at *CallReview*, and Chris Danowski, editor of *Performing the Here and Now*. New Dramatists in New York City played a role in a spiritual and practical way with the play's life. To all the artists at Woodshed Collective and to The Jones Street Boys, heartfelt thanks. As always, this is for my parents.

'Resurrections:
The Work of Caridad Svich'

How do you make facts out of dreams?
You write plays. If you're Caridad
Svich, the plays you write arrive trailing
the filament of those dreams, like
seaweed off a drowned girl. The plays
thrum with the music of those dreams,
half remembered, old songs remixed by
their collision with the waking world.
They describe passage from dream into
dream, nightmare into nightmare, past
ruin into present wreckage. They
attempt, to use Caridad's powerful,
enigmatic phrase from the title of one of
her plays, to "steal back light from the
virtual."

Caridad's facts are resurrections
and, as such, they seem both other-
worldly and this worldly, stratified by
time and loss. "The world lays itself
down in layers," says the actor Edwin in
The Booth Variations, written with Todd
Cerveris, "one on top of the other. One
shot, another, one boy, another." It is

Civil War America, just before Edwin's brother will shoot the President. "I am field of men on a broken land. I am grey luminous flares across the southern sky. I am the membrane of a newly-divided country, torn, torn, and return." Matthew Brady, who will capture these fields of men so beautifully on photographic plates, might be defining Caridad's own project as an artist when he says, "I make cathedrals out of carnage."

So many of her facts are actual resurrections—of ancient, buried, beloved, untranslated, almost lost or nearly forgotten texts—and in this way it has seemed to me that Caridad plays the role of community spiritualist, holding séances to summon or channel the dead—Euripides, Shakespeare, Lope de Vega, Calderon, and Lorca. And so the layers continue, as she calls up these spirits and, most often, crashes them into the contemporary or beyond, marrying her polar obsessions—great works of the past and the culture of young now and in some the virtual future. Throughout her work, the already dead and the soon-dead walk together, the damned and the doomed. They are what she calls, in her version of *Medea*, "flesh and blood apparitions." And they walk, wounded, in a ravaged world, even if, in the classical plays set among the ruling classes, it is fabulous wreckage.

Iphigenia Crash Land Falls on the Neon Shell that Was Once Her Heart is a rave adaptation of the Greek tragedy of Iphigenia, the general's daughter who was sacrificed so that the Greeks could sail to Troy. This time we are in an unnamed South American country, among the brutal, corrupt, and sexually ambiguous, where children of the wealthy are kidnapped and disappeared, and dead Fresa girls dance. In Caridad land, we move like specters, starved for sensation, love, sex, ready for a glorious sacrifice, ready to be fucked by our fate, as if this sacrifice were religious, Christ-like, world redeeming. And as we move through this world, this trans-global, boundary-less, everywhere nowhere world, we never land, never rest. It is the immigrant's wandering, the hyphenate's homelessness, or as she puts it in her play *Prodigal Kiss*, "This I without a name, without a country/This spectral I who roams the land/Escaping from wounds newly bled." But in the new millennium, the exile is macroscopic, our restlessness has metastasized. There is no home, past or future, here or there. And in a sense, there is no self, only performance.

Todd London
Artistic Director, New Dramatists, NY

On the Making of

12 Ophelias (a play with broken songs):

Caridad Svich in conversation with Joe
Filippazzo.

This e-mail interview was conducted in
June 2008 during rehearsals for the
Woodshed Collective site-responsive
premiere of *12 Ophelias* at McCarren
Park Pool.

**First give me some background: Where
are you from? Where do you live?
What do you do for a living? Etc.**

I was born in Philadelphia, PA. Grew up
in Bethelem, PA; Paterson, NJ; Miami,
FL; Salt Lake City, UT; Charlotte, NC;
San Diego, CA. I'm of Cuban-
Spanish/Argentine-Croatian
background. Bilingual household
(Spanish-English). I became interested
in theatre and performance early on, but
writing has always been part of my
creative expression. In college trained as

actor-singer and then went to graduate school at UCSD and rec'd my MFA in Playwriting. After that studied with Maria Irene Fornes for four consecutive years at INTAR in NY, after which she directed my play *Any Place But Here* at Theater for the New City. I've lived, in my adult life, mostly in California, New York, Ohio, and Massachusetts. Over the last several years I've split my time between NY and Los Angeles fairly consistently but a great deal more time spent in NY. I make my living as a playwright, theatrical translator, arts journalist, editor and educator.

The play ran at Baruch College in New York City in 2004 for a few performances, but how do you think it fits into the Brooklyn setting at McCarren Park Pool?
The play ran for a couple of performances at Baruch Performing Arts Center in 2004 under the direction of Debbie Saivetz with a company of actors compromised of professionals (some of which had been instrumental

in the play's development: Michael Gladis, Alfredo Narciso, Alex Oliver, Chris Wells) and students with a musical score written by myself with additional settings by Michael Gladis and Michael Ray Escamilla. Previously to BPAC the play was developed at Powerhouse Theatre/NY Stage and Film, Red Bull Theater, and New Georges. Although the play was presented at BPAC, the show was not open to the press. The 2008 Woodshed Collective production is its premiere.

In terms of its setting at McCarren Park Pool, first of all I'm thrilled that this is the first play ever to be presented at McCarren Park Pool. Here's a play that is watery in nature, a play about ruin and rising from ruin, a play with songs, a play rooted in a history but also claimed into a new history, being performed in a pool with a rich performance history (Gogol Bordello, Wilco, The Hold Steady, DJ Shadow, M.I.A., etc.), a strong relationship to its community and neighborhood, and the memory of water in its "ghostly bones." When Woodshed Collective approached me about doing *12 Ophelias*, the conversation soon turned to how the play could live in a natural setting, and when McCarren Park Pool was secured as venue, it felt as if a fortuitous serendipitous dialogue would arise between the text and the space. I have a strong interest in working in nontraditional, site specific spaces and in making site-responsive work, and in exploring the relationship between text and audiences in different ways; the fact that this play has found professional life in this manner is very much a continuation of my own artistic concerns.

Have you worked with the Woodshed Collective before?
This is the first time I've worked with Woodshed Collective, but we've been in intense conversations for about a year about my works. I've also worked with company members Jocelyn Kuritsky on

several projects (as one of my actors) and with Stephen Squibb (as dramaturg), so there's been a strong connection to Woodshed Collective for a while.

When did you write *12 Ophelias*? How did you come up with the concept?

I wrote the play initially in 2002 and then kept working on it til 2004, and then some more now in 2008 for this production. I'd written a hybrid adaptation of Shakespeare's *Winter's Tale* entitled *Perdita Gracia* when I was the Jonathan R Reynolds Playwright in Residence at Denison University in Granville Ohio. From 2001-2004 I co-conceived, created and co-wrote the multimedia collaboration *The Booth Variations* with actor Todd Cerveris and director Nick Philippou (the show premiered at 59 East 59 in 2004 and Edinburgh Fringe Festival in 2005) and this piece used as central focus our deconstruction of *Hamlet*. So, I was rather in a Shakespeare phase. The idea for *12 Ophelias* came at first from living with the deconstructed Hamlet in *The Booth Variations* for so long; it ignited in me a fascination with Ophelia's voice and a desire to render it in a different way. So many visual artists, poets and dramatists over the centuries have taken Ophelia's story on - not surprisingly. She is one of Shakespeare's most troubled and enigmatic young women - good daughter, good sister, lover, touched by/driven to madness, suicide. A tragic case felled by one society and story and thus it's inevitable that there seems to be a constant need to retrieve her from her fate as dramatic figure. My desire was indeed to rescue her, resuscitate her language, and find a new language and place for her to land in my own way. This desire has also fueled other hybrid re-imaginings I've written: *Iphigenia Crash Land Falls on the Neon Shell That Was Once Her Heart (a rave fable)*, *Antigone Arkhe* [as part of *The Antigone Project*], *Wreckage* [from Euripides' *Medea*], *Lucinda Caval* [also riffing on Antigone], *Lulu Ascending* [contemporary riff on Wedekind's *Pandora's Box*], and even to some extent *Steal Back Light from the Virtual* [which uses the myth of the Minotaur and Ariadne and the thread as central motif]. In *12 Ophelias*, I wanted to re-animate Ophelia's desires and explore her fragmented memories so that she can leave them behind for once and for all and walk upon this earth anew. I also wanted to create a living theatre song-poem, a hybrid form that would allow the remnants of Shakespearean language to brush up, caress and collide with a new language steeped in a memory-drenched, invented idiom recalled from Appalachian ballads, laments and hymns: a rubbed off sepia-scope of sound and memory. So, I began to write the text and songs (lyrics and music) in tandem, and the play and the songs came to be.

Talk about the musical accompaniment in this and your plays in general.

I trained originally as a pianist-guitarist and singer; primarily as a singer and have always written songs. Many of my plays use songs in a central and essential manner and I do think of them as hybrid new music-theatre pieces, really. For me the spoken word is also part of the score. In fact the whole play is a score to be played/performed. I don't really think of music as being separate from speech. Everything stems from breath, from vocalization, the voice lifted in space through time. I've been greatly influenced by Shakespeare, Lorca, and Brecht in the theatre but also by the songs of so many amazing songwriters in pop music - songwriters who write pieces that sometimes feel like mini theatre pieces: Aimee Mann, Tom Waits, Lou Reed, David Bowie, Prince, the Real Tuesday Weld, Rufus Wainwright, Arcade Fire, the Divine Comedy, and so many more.

I'd written the musical settings to my lyrics for this play between 2002 and 2004. Along the way actor-musicians

Michael Gladis and Michael Ray Escamilla became part of the play's development and I wrote lyrics to two new songs especially so that they could set them. By 2004 when the BPAC staging took place, that score had been set. But I'm always interested as a songwriter to offer my lyrics to other composers to set (this has been true of other plays with songs I've written, among them *Alchemy of Desire/Dead-Man's Blues, Fugitive Pieces, Prodigal Kiss, Thrush, and Iphigenia...a rave fable.* The sound of *12 Ophelias* has always been intentionally neo-roots Americana based. A nouveau Appalachia sound full of plaintive chords, high lonesome cries, bluesy riffs, and ancient-feeling register.

When Woodshed Collective approached me about the possibility of new musical settings for this production and The Jones Street Boys' interest in setting the lyrics, I thought their sound as a band and my words would make a great fit. I loved the idea of this terrific neo-roots/bluegrass Brooklyn-based band being part of the world of this play and the professional premiere at McCarren Park Pool.

Do you think that the play would appeal to people who are unfamiliar with Hamlet?

The play is about being broken by society and love, about being lost and about finding yourself again. I think anyone who's experienced profound heartbreak would connect to this play. A knowledge or familiarity with *Hamlet* is not necessarily a prerequisite.

12 OPHELIAS

(a play with broken songs)

12 Ophelias at McCarren Park Pool
Photo courtesy of Woodshed Collective (2008)

Script History

This script was developed at Powerhouse Theater/New York Stage and Film, and later at New Georges, and Red Bull Theater in New York City. It was presented at Baruch Performing Arts Center in New York City under the direction of Debbie Saivetz in April 2004, with original music composed by the author with Michael Escamilla and Michael Gladis. The principal roles were played by: Heather Starkel (Ophelia), Michael Gladis (Rude Boy). Alfredo Narciso (H), Chris Wells (G), Alex Oliver (G), Kristi Casey (Gertrude), Alissa Ford (Mina). Design team was comprised of Steve O'Shea, Jessica Gaffney, and Ariadne Condos. Choreography was by Tracy Bersley, stage manager was Pamela Salling.

The play received its professional premiere in a site-responsive production by Woodshed Collective at McCarren Park Pool on July 24, 2008. It was directed by Teddy Bergman; the set design was by Gabe Evansohn; the costume design was by Jessica Pabst; dance/movement choreography by Nicola Bullock; fight choreography by Adam Rihacek, musical direction by Emily Fishbaine; and original music composed by The Jones Street Boys.

Ellen Shadburn was the stage manager, and the line producer for Woodshed Collective was Stephen Squibb. The production publicist was Richard Kornberg of Richard Kornberg & Associates. The cast was as follows:

Ophelia...............Pepper Binkley	
RudeBoy............Dan Cozzens	
R.................	Grace McLean
G....................	Preston G. Martin
H...............	Ben Beckley
Gertrude......	Kate Benson
Mina...............	Jocelyn Kuritsky
Chorus (of Ophelias)...	The Jones Street Boys

A previous version of this text is published in *Performing the Here and Now: An Introduction to Contemporary Theater and Performance* (Kendall/Hunt Publishing, 2005), and also in the independent literary journal *CallReview* (Issue #2, 2004); a first edition of the text was made available from NoPassport Press for the duration of the run at McCarren Park Pool.

An audio/visual multimedia feature of the Woodshed Collective production is archived by *The New York Times* at http://www.nytimes.com/interactive/2008/07/25/theater/twelve-ophelias3/index.html

Shakespeare's Ophelia rises up out of the water dreaming of Pop-Tarts and other sweet things. She finds herself in a neo-Elizabethan Appalachian setting where Gertrude runs a brothel, Hamlet is called a Rude Boy, and nothing is what it seems. In this mirrored world of word-scraps and cold sex, Ophelia cuts a new path for herself.

To see what I'm seeing,
you have to look.
--anonymous

"This is the very ecstasy of love,
whose violent property fordoes itself..."
--Polonius to Ophelia,
Act II, scene 1, *Hamlet*

Characters:

OPHELIA, cracked angel for a new-fangled age

RUDE BOY (Hamlet), Ophelia's undisguised lover

R (Rosencrantz), guardian of memory, androgynous, (preferably played by a woman)

G (Guildenstern), guardian of memory, androgynous (preferably played by a man); also plays OPHELIA's DOUBLE

H (Horatio), best friend and confidante of Rude Boy

GERTRUDE, a monied madam with a pure voice

MINA, local whore

CHORUS OF OPHELIAS, five apparitions, voices buried underwater*

The Setting:

Water. Road. Time.

Notes:

The chorus may be live or heard/seen as
pre-recorded voices.

Melodies to the original songs featured
in the text may be obtained by
contacting the author, or lyrics may be
re-set by another composer.

One

OPHELIA rises up out of the water. She wears a garland of crushed flowers and dreams of ring pops, sugar pops, popsicles, sweet things. She is full of craving. She is nothing but want. She sings.

"Be fallen"

OPHELIA: Fall and be fallen
All around is sky
Deep eternal winter
For a muted sigh.

Fall and be fallen
All around is sky
Deep eternal winter
For a muted sigh

She speaks.

Something in my mouth to have
or soon no more.
Name carved on tree, skin, breath.

Think what that does to a girl,
to a sorry lonesome thing
left by her boy.
Left to be a-drowned.
It burns her up it does. It sends her ruin.
Time is the cruelest revelator.
I had me an angel.
He was sweet and turned swervy.
I should have known then…
but fool mind, fool heart…
what that does to a body
cannot be accounted.
So I went into water.
I scooped up the living.
And made promises to the dead.
I left everyone unblessed.
I jangled a laugh and a song of sorrow,
a tall, lonesome song
you could hear through the wildflowers.
I sang me Jesus
and made everyone a-scared
and regretful for their sins.
My name became legend.
Cries asunder all over the valley:
"Ophelia was our daughter.
We done her a wrong turn.

Never to be done again."
The song echoed.
And I was atoned under bubble tones,
under water.
Then everything forgotten.
Years. And a girl is just a story,
and a woman's shame is un-felt,
and the boy grows up
with a cruel mouth
and a vindictive heart,
and feels no remorse
for what he has done.
It's paying time. I feel it.
The boy will remember.
I am on land.
I am become bewildered,
but soon, soon , soon
a wanting taste.
Honey from trees inside my belly.
Wretched Ophelia will be no more.

Two

R and G watch the water as if it were porcelain fabric. They wash lingerie.

R: It awful, in't? That Ophelia girl, thinking she's so… every girl is put upon. She got to learn that.

G: Not easy to learn.

R: High church, she is. Coming back here. What for?

G: Find her man.

R: Lost love?

G: Not lost on me.

R: A wrecker. A mad one. A selfish beast.

G: Dressed like a prince.

R: Hamlet?

G: Yeh.

R: Dresses fine. Like a lad. He's nothing but.

G: The laddish ones always get girls heads turned round, don't they?

R: They got ways and means.

G: Don't want the likes of them on me.

R: No lust in your heart, G?

G: Plenty of lust, but pain, too. What am I do with it?

R: Bury it. Cover it up. That's what all women do.

G: Does me no good.

R: Forget.

G: Yeh. I like forgetting. It's easeful.

R: Remembering is a bother.

G: Brings everything up: hurt and criminal things.

R: What's done is done.

G: Right said.

Beat.

R: You think he's seen her?

G: What does Hamlet see?

R: Sees what he wants. True enough. Can't see past himself.

G: He's filled up with his own thoughts. You think he's thought a moment about her?

R: Cries enough.

G: Cried once. To make a show of his feeling. Not true. Never was. Not to Ophelia.

R: He's a rude one.

G: They all are.

R: Men, you mean?

G: Everyone. But him in particular.

R: You got hate for him.

G: Wanted me killed, didn't he? Wanted us both killed: "R and G. See that they're hanged." After all we'd done for him.

R: That's in the past.

G: Ancient law. Another life. That's right. But the feeling remains. People thirst for a good hanging.

R: He's not the same.

G: The Rude boy? He's still Hamlet.

R: Revenge in his heart.

G: He's got a bad inheritance. They're all twisted in that family. Every one of them. Full of themselves. Thinking nothing of what's around them. Acting like they do, like they're intentions are honorable. Nothing but crap.

R: Does nothing to mean well.

G: Right said.

Beat.

Look at the water. Like it could crack it's so smooth.

R: It's like an ivory pitcher.

G: Is it?

R: Is to me. Smooth and fine. Like I had in my house once. Sat on a tapletop.

Ivory pitcher filled with milk. Calming to look at.

G: Not to go in, though.

R: This here? No. I don't like cold water. I like the sea. The Caribbean, the Mediterranean. Warm things. Cold's shivery, and hostile to life.

G: IS life, some say.

R: Not to me. Shivers are not my idea of living.
...How'd Ophelia do it? Eh? Come up like that from water chaste as ice?

G: She must have been floating.

R: Must have been very still.

G: The water released her.

R: Like a stem.

G: And there was nothing she could do.

R: Must have been wanting…

G: Ophelia?

R: For a long time, must've been…
waiting for the water, for the slip
through and coming up for air.

G: Only to come back here. Shame.

R: Curse.

G: Yeh. Ophelia's got that.

R: Could get rid of it.

G: What's inside her, what's been bred?

R: Change is possible.

G: Change is a fool's mission. There is
no change. World is crap rotten, always
has been. Sun is a gash on the planet.
We scoop it up cause we've no choice.
What's Ophelia going to change?

R: Her heart.

Three

*Edge of road. Ophelia sees herself framed in
the RUDE BOY's glance. He sings.*

"Look Now"

RUDE BOY
Look now
Brave in despair
Treacherous girl
Seek to follow me

Bend down
Upon my swoon
Upon my reed
Made for your need

Look now
Brave in delight
Decorous girl
Seek to follow me

Rest your tears
Upon my soft pillow

Let me wrap you
In mordant bliss.

She beckons him.

OPHELIA: What I got in me cannot be filled.

RUDE BOY: You were a-drowned.

OPHELIA: I was a mermaid. Did you see me?

RUDE BOY: Wet's what I see.

OPHELIA: …Come to me.

RUDE BOY: Strange girl.

OPHELIA: Hand over fist. Make me lesser.

RUDE BOY: You are sent down from the moon.

OPHELIA: I know not the moon, but when it shines upon me I am humble made.

RUDE BOY: Is it right to want so much?

OPHELIA: Honey drips. Catch me.

Beat.

RUDE BOY: What are you made of?

OPHELIA: Long purple stems.

RUDE BOY: Made to be cut?

OPHELIA: If you wish…

RUDE BOY: What else?

OPHELIA: Acid leaves.

RUDE BOY: On your tongue?

OPHELIA: Deep inside me.

RUDE BOY: You should be ashamed.

OPHELIA: I am blasted with ecstasy.

RUDE BOY: You'll be found out.

OPHELIA: No one knows I'm here,
except you.

RUDE BOY: You've been loosed?

OPHELIA: Out of water I've stepped
out, unseen by mortal eye. I've walked
dripping sweet upon the cold earth and
caught you looking at me.

RUDE BOY: That's talk.

OPHELIA: That's what we're made of.

RUDE BOY: I'm not.

OPHELIA: What are you made of?

RUDE BOY: Flesh. Bone. Muscle.

OPHELIA: Show me your fist.

RUDE BOY: I'm strong.

OPHELIA: I can take.

RUDE BOY: You have soft hands.

OPHELIA: To redeem you.

RUDE BOY: Is that a threat?

OPHELIA: It's whatever you make of it.

RUDE BOY: Where'd you come from?

OPHELIA: Here.

RUDE BOY: Never seen you.

OPHELIA: You're seeing me now.

RUDE BOY: The question is

OPHELIA: Do you like what you see?

RUDE BOY: Yeah.

OPHELIA: What's not to like about me?

RUDE BOY: Don't know.

OPHELIA: Hah.

RUDE BOY: Hah.

Beat.

OPHELIA: We're the same.

RUDE BOY: We're not.

OPHELIA: We think alike.

RUDE BOY: If that's what you'd like to think.

OPHELIA: I do not know what I should think. Tell me.

RUDE BOY: Don't know you. Can't offer anything.

OPHELIA: Offer skin.

RUDE BOY: Yeah.

OPHELIA: Offer smile.

RUDE BOY: Yeah.

OPHELIA: Offer what you will.

RUDE BOY: What I will. Nothing more.

OPHELIA: Fair enough.

RUDE BOY: Is it?

OPHELIA: Love's fair.

RUDE BOY: Are you in love?

OPHELIA: Don't know. I like, though.
Like you.

RUDE BOY: Don't know me.

OPHELIA: See you. That's enough.

RUDE BOY: Looks are deceiving.

OPHELIA: How's that?

RUDE BOY: Can't trust what you see. Things change on you in a wink blink.

OPHELIA: Then what?

RUDE BOY: Then you're damned.

OPHELIA: Is that the story?

RUDE BOY: Round here. Yeah.

OPHELIA: Strange place, this. Strange air. Sticks to you. Cold wind.

RUDE BOY: From the water. From the north. Everything swoops through here. It goes, though. After a while, you don't feel it.

OPHELIA: You forget.

RUDE BOY: Get used to things. That's how it is. You live someplace, you get used to pretty much everything.

OPHELIA: Lies?

RUDE BOY: Yeah.

OPHELIA: Madness?

RUDE BOY: Common everyday. That's what things become.

OPHELIA: What about me?

RUDE BOY: Well, you're new, aren't you?

OPHELIA: I'm plenty.

RUDE BOY: Yeah. You're ripe. No question. I could teach you bout this place.

OPHELIA: Will you?

RUDE BOY: I don't mind.

Beat.

OPHELIA: What should I call you, then?

RUDE BOY: Name me.

OPHELIA: …Hamlet.

RUDE BOY: He's no one.

OPHELIA: He loves me. He's cruel.

RUDE BOY: Yeah. But we all are. That's survival, in't? You get what you make, reap what you sow, that sort of thing.

OPHELIA: Words.

RUDE BOY: Don't you like them?

OPHELIA: I like their edges.

RUDE BOY: Take them.

OPHELIA: You think I just take and don't put up a fight? You must think I'm one sorry thing.

RUDE BOY: I don't think anything.

OPHELIA: Hollow brain?

RUDE BOY: I try not to put too much in it.

OPHELIA: What do you go by?

RUDE BOY: You want a name?

OPHELIA: I like having something to hold onto.

RUDE BOY: Ain't got one.

OPHELIA: What'd you mean?

RUDE BOY: I'm rude. Down to my skivvies.

OPHELIA: A rude boy?

RUDE BOY: Nothing else to me.

OPHELIA: You are in disguise.

RUDE BOY: If you want.

OPHELIA: Yes. I want. I want pure full of mercy thoughts that will make their way into me and release me from penitence.

RUDE BOY: That's a huge want. Don't know I can give that.

OPHELIA: Why not? You think I'm good? I'm not. Never have been. Fate has played a part and I've been willing, that's all. I've let a story be spun cause it suited me and my purpose once. But no more. No longer. Come now in your disguise. Be rude. Be who you are. I won't seek forgiveness.

They kiss.

RUDE BOY: What's your name again?

OPHELIA: Ophelia.

Four

*GERTRUDE watches Ophelia and the Rude
Boy make love. She sings.*

"Calling"

GERTRUDE: Dead men call on the maid
Call on the maid with the long purple
Wrap them with fingers cold as a blade
Patient as a dove
I see her face

*In the distance,
the Chorus of Ophelias joins her in song.*

CHORUS: Woe unto the child

GERTRUDE: She looks my way

CHORUS & GERTRUDE: Haunted
devil…

GERTRUDE: Dead men take from the maid

CHORUS & GERTRUDE: Take from the maid what they're needing

GERTRUDE: Leave them with bellies open in shame…

GERTRUDE & CHORUS: Tender as a dove.

Ophelia is left by the Rude Boy. R and G discover Ophelia, scoop her up, and take her to Gertrude's place.

Five

Some time later.

GERTRUDE: Love grows aslant. Nothing to be done.

R: She's been cut.

G: Bled through.

GERTRUDE: She's nothing to me.

R: Rude boy done her strange.

GERTRUDE: She looked for him, didn't she?

G: Didn't deserve to be cut.

GERTRUDE: No one should expect anything in this world. Not kindness, nothing tender. You expect? You get.

G: Not knife, though. That's not worth getting.

GERTRUDE: What do you want me to do?

R: See her. Give her a place.

GERTRUDE: Here?

R: Look after her a bit until she's... you know...

GERTRUDE: Don't know.

R: Just look after her. An afternoon. Evening. A bit of tending will do her all right.

GERTRUDE: Why don't you?

R: Ain't got.

G: None of us have.

R: No place.

GERTRUDE: Sorry creatures.

R & G: We are.

GERTRUDE: That's why you come to me.

R: All the sorrys. That's right. We beg and bow.

Beat.

GERTRUDE: Where is she?

R: You'll treat her right?

GERTRUDE: What do you take me for?

G: Gertrude.

GERTRUDE: Is that how you come to me? With mean-ness? I won't do anyone right if right's not given me.

G: Gertrude.

GERTRUDE: That's better.

G: As if you'd know the difference.

GERTRUDE: What'd you say?

G: Nothing at all.

R: G's taken to mumbling.

GERTRUDE: I don't like mumbling.

G: Don't like anything, do you?

GERTRUDE: What's that?

G: You've got pot of money, that's what. We kneel, don't we?

GERTRUDE: Fake diamonds, fake everything. I'm just show.

G: Show pony?

GERTRUDE: Pin-up girl. That's me.

R: Wouldn't we give....?

GERTRUDE: Wouldn't everybody...
Come on now. Lead me to her. Let's see
the poor thing.

Ophelia is seen.

OPHELIA: Not not, not want touch. Not
here. Right? Ain't right. See?

GERTRUDE: Been left, have you? Is that
the story?

OPHELIA: Nothing nobody, got no
thought, swimming like, that's me, I
swim through, I float, I cling to an edge
where there's not one, I've got plenty,
nobody leaves me.

GERTRUDE
Got cut down the belly?

OPHELIA: Cut myself. Did justice.
Didn't want anything growing in me.

GERTRUDE: Don't give me lip. I won't have it. Word's out. You've been left. Sad story, but true, cause that's what we make of stories: sad pitiful things we carry with us for comfort's sake. You want a hug and a tear, you're not getting it from me. Let's see the wound.

Ophelia reveals.

OPHELIA: He stuck the blade in me, the rude boy, as if he'd been loosed out of hell; he was looking for blood while I was sleeping.

GERTRUDE: That's something I can believe. The Rude Boy wrongs everyone.

G: He does.

OPHELIA: Good story, then?

GERTRUDE: It serves.

OPHELIA: What purpose I know not.

GERTRUDE: What'd you mean?

OPHELIA: Nothing. Words. They come out like... spirit things.

GERTRUDE: You best watch them. Words should be measured, not spilt.

OPHELIA: Is that your story?

GERTRUDE: No story to me. I'm Gertrude. That's all.

OPHELIA: Damned one.

GERTRUDE: Who said that?

OPHELIA: 'Tis in my memory locked.

GERTRUDE: I think you've lost a little too much blood. You're starting to imagine things.

OPHELIA: What's to imagine?

*R and G enact a scene from Ophelia's
fractured memory. R speaks as Hamlet
might; G speaks as Ophelia would. This is a
version of the "nunnery" scene from* Hamlet
played with the precision of a broken clock.

R: …The fair Ophelia!
Nymph, in thy orisons
Be all my sins remember'd.

G :My lord, I have remembrances of
yours, That I have longed long to re-
deliver;

R : Ha, ha! are you honest?

G : My lord?

R : Are you fair?

G: What means your lordship?

R: I did love you once.

G : You made me believe so.

R : You should not have believed me. I loved you not.

G : Words of so sweet breath: their perfume lost. I am deceived.

Beat.

R: What should such fellows as I do, crawling between earth and heaven?

G: Love, and in that love, make me believe.

R: I am the more deceived.

Beat.

G: If I could interpret your love.

R: You will have found me out.

G: Strange paradox.

R: Stranger for being true. Time
will have its proof.

G: I am a slave to memory.

R: And I could accuse me of such
things that it were better my
mother had not borne me.

Beat.

G: O heavenly powers, restore him.

R: You nickname God's creatures and
make wanton-ness your ignorance.

G: My honoured lord. I have
remembrances of yours.

R: I did love you once.

G: You know right well you did.

R : You should not have believed me. I loved you not.

G: Wound me.

R: To the quick, and with such strength I'll show you a thorny way to heaven.

G: Out of tune and harsh....

R: Know this to be true: what you see is an errant translation of my heart. Make me a monster. And thus never wretched will you be.

G: Wound me again, for I see what I see.

R and G are caught in a repeated gesture of love's wounding nature.

Wound me again, for I see what I see.
Wound me again, for I see what I see.
Wound me again, for I see what I see.
Wound me again, for I see what I see.

End of fractured memory.

OPHELIA: You imagine much, you two.

R & G: Do we?

OPHELIA: But you do not remember everything.

GERTRUDE: What?

OPHELIA: These two. They've got wild history in them.

GERTRUDE: They're always acting. …Useless. Aren't you?

R & G: We're fools.

GERTRUDE: And the better for it. Intelligence is the ruin of most people.

OPHELIA: You mean knowledge?

GERTRUDE: Intelligence, perceptiveness, insight: ruin. Smarts are what you need. They get you through.

OPHELIA: Not books.

GERTRUDE: Books are a joke. Waste of paper. Stories made up to distract people, that's all they are. I read me a magazine. Does me fine. Get the highlights, a bit of the news, find out what's going on in the world, and some beauty advice. I've got everything I need, for what paper can give me. Ink. You understand?

OPHELIA: Ink stains.

GERTRUDE: That's right. It leaves a mark. …You've a surface cut, from what I can tell. Looks deeper than it is. You've lost blood but you could've lost more.

OPHELIA: Lay your hands on me?

GERTRUDE: You think I'm a healer?

OPHELIA: Just do. Need.

GERTRUDE: You say things with such a face.

OPHELIA: You find me worthy of pity?

GERTRUDE: I don't like pitying anyone. It's a mess of a feeling. You should break your habit.

OPHELIA: What'd you mean?

R: Stop acting wretched, that's what.

OPHELIA: I'm not acting.

G: You mean you are wretched? Truly?

OPHELIA: No.

R: Then what are you talking, girl?

GERTRUDE: Wretchedness is unbecoming. Best way to get trampled is to act like you've been trampled. The smart ones eye you in a second, and waste no time ravaging, cause that's what they do, that's what they like. Everyone's under foot to them.

OPHELIA: Feels better.

GERTRUDE: My hands?

OPHELIA: Yeah. Angel like.

GERTRUDE: That's enough then.

Beat.

OPHELIA: He was rude.

GERTRUDE: What?

OPHELIA: The boy met by the field. The beauteous one with the cold heart. I said to him: you are, you are, you are to me what a bird is to a tree, a place to nest.

GERTRUDE: Those words are not to be said.

OPHELIA: Didn't know.

GERTRUDE: Ignorant, are you?

OPHELIA: Don't know. Seen plenty.
Done plenty. Got a mess of history in
me. Wronged is my state. Always have
been. I'm a wronged girl.

GERTRUDE: You're a woman. There are
no girls here.

OPHELIA: Them.

GERTRUDE: R and G? They ain't girls.

OPHELIA: Seem it.

GERTRUDE: They're dressed but there's
not a girl thing to them. They're as rude
as your boy.

OPHELIA: Are they?

R & G: We are as named.

OPHELIA: Trick of the eyes, then.

GERTRUDE: Trick in everything here. This place is full of mirrors, and shifting lenses. There are traps where you least expect.

OPHELIA: You'll take care of me, then?

GERTRUDE: I'll put you up for a night. You need a change of clothes, a bit of healing. Nothing that can't be fixed, dove. Take what caring comes to you. You don't know if it'll ever come to you again.

OPHELIA: You used to cry when you heard my name.

GERTRUDE: Me?

OPHELIA: I remember. You used to sing

She sings to the melody of the opening two lines of "Calling."

"Ophelia, find her a way.
Find her a hole to be buried."

GERTRUDE: What are you talking about?

OPHELIA: From my before life I remember.

GERTRUDE: Before? Now's all there is. You're living out of some story. I'm Gertrude. A rich whore. Nothing else to me.

OPHELIA: My mind's muddy.

GERTRUDE: Have you et?

OPHELIA: I'd like something swirly.

GERTRUDE: Sugar pop?

OPHELIA: It's got a good sound, don't it?

GERTRUDE: Like an ad.

OPHELIA: Sugar, sugar, sugar pop.

GERTRUDE: Pop til you drop.

OPHELIA: …You think my heart is any lesser?

GERTRUDE: What'd you mean?

OPHELIA: For being born?

GERTRUDE: I think you're born with who you'll be inside of you. Nothing can change that. Not even being re-born. A rude boy will be rude. A woman will be wronged. A country will keep going. You're looking for something else? You'll have to be sent down from another moon.

Gertrude takes Ophelia by the hand. They walk away. R and G follow.

Six

Rude Boy revels in his fortune with H. They wrestle as is their common practice.

RUDE BOY: Fuck what did her a feverish wow you should've seen.

H: Is that where you've been?

RUDE BOY: Screwing. What else?

H: Didn't tell me.

RUDE BOY: Didn't know I'd do.

H: Was she sweet?

RUDE BOY: Give a finger.

H: I'm serious. Was she?

RUDE BOY: Dripping everything. Ain't seen her like in a while. Pure eyes, chastened heart. Unashamed of her scarlet pulse.

H: Whore, then?

RUDE BOY: No. Not a bit. Called herself a mermaid. A watery figure ready to be transformed.

H: Book type?

RUDE BOY: Had enough of books, she said. Had her right fill. No more reading for her. Making life instead.

H: Book types are always book types. They don't change. Best watch yourself. They're the worst kind. Their heads are full of stories and they want to act them out, and there's no end to them.

RUDE BOY: You're a pout.

H: I'm not.

RUDE BOY: You miss me, H?

H: I ain't a fag.

RUDE BOY: Never said, but what of it? You're pouting just the same. Jealous, are you?

H: Of your lay? Don't need a new one. Got Mina, Gertrude's girl. She's all right for me.

RUDE BOY: Mina's garbage.

H: Hey.

RUDE BOY: She is. Tell me she's not. Sucking on sugar pop all the time, inhaling things, she's got a shattered anatomy.

H: She feeds. Sustains herself. I don't see what's wrong with that.

RUDE BOY: You like her cause she's always at the ready.

H: No drama, if that's what you mean. I don't like conflict. It's unnecessary. Life's simple. We get on, then what's the worry? We get on with it. No "if you please, and what's anyone going to think." Sick of roundabout. My feelings, her feelings. What of them? You spend so much time being cautious of each other's feelings, deal's done and you're in a potter's field, and then what? I won't have it. Mina's good for me.

RUDE BOY: Not in love.

H: I don't throw that word about.

RUDE BOY: I see.

H: ...What? You're going to tell me...?

RUDE BOY: I'm not.

H: Is that what this is?

RUDE BOY: Not a bit.

H: You've fallen for this one?

RUDE BOY: You know I don't fall. Did that once. Cost me.

H: I remember.

RUDE BOY: Through with love.

H: That's what you said.

RUDE BOY: Just debating about…

H: In your head?

RUDE BOY: She's soft on me, and I'm soft…and truth can come clean.

H: Who is this woman that's turned you around?

RUDE BOY: Ophelia.

H: That's a cursed name.

RUDE BOY: I know. But she's different.

H: You're mooning. In the sky.

RUDE BOY: I can't tell you anything.

H: I've known you since school days. You can tell me everything, but not about love, not this one. Cause you screwed her? What of it? She's just another. You promised you wouldn't fall again.

RUDE BOY: Stupid promise.

H: Best thing you ever did. You're no good at love.

RUDE BOY: What'd you mean?

H: Hopeless.

RUDE BOY: That's a rotten thing…

H: I speak true. You ruin everything with your temper.

RUDE BOY: I haven't got temper.

H: Ready fists. Knife in pocket. Looking for a brawl.

RUDE BOY: I've an agile mind.

H: Do you use it?

RUDE BOY: Do you want to spoil things? Is that your job? I speak what I'm thinking, you twist everything about.

H: Fight me, then.

RUDE BOY: I don't get you. You're content with Mina? Be content. I don't mind. But what about me? You ever think?

H: You'll never be content.

RUDE BOY: Cause I'm a rude one?

H: You're what you are.

RUDE BOY: Change is possible.

H: How are you going to change?

RUDE BOY: Better myself, what's inside me.

H: Won't happen.

RUDE BOY: I thought you had faith in me.

H: I do. Always have. But you're a wrecker. That's a fact. You destroy, sometimes without meaning. Fear's in you. You think too much of yourself. You push people away.

RUDE BOY: Won't with this one.

H: How do you know?

RUDE BOY: I've learned from the past.

H: What is learned can't be unlearned. You can't help your nature.

RUDE BOY: Nature's form holds me; in which glass do I see?

H: Mine.

They jab at each other until they fall to the ground, worn and fatigued from wrestling. R and G come upon them...

R: Filled with it, eh?

G: Rude one. Yeh.

R: Filled with promise.

G: To what end?

R: Love's end.

G: Speak true.

R: I do.

G: Turned about, you are.

R: Am not.

G: Thinking the Rude one will…?

R: Change. Yes. He loves her now.

G: Always did.

R: Loves her more.

G: Makes good show of it.

R: You think love's a game?

G: I never said…

R: You think, though.

G: I think he thinks as much. What's he done? Not much that I can see. Cut her, didn't he?

R: Don't know bout that.

G: You say he didn't?

R: Stories get told. Don't mean nothing.

G: Stories true bleed eternally.
Counterfeit love wears brilliant conceit.

R: Quiet now. They rest.

G: In the sweet flowers they lay – the
rude bothered and his noble mate.

R: In love's expectancy.

G: In fashion's fatigue.

R: Blown youth.

G: In bold serenity.

Seven

Evening. Ophelia sings to nobody.

"Cut to be Whole"

OPHELIA: To speak of horrors he
comes before me
a-burnin, in disguise

In the distance, chorus of Ophelias joins her]

CHORUS & OPHELIA: Cut to be whole,
truth a-seekin
Soft as a lover's lies

OPHELIA: Soft on breeze
his whisper dreams me
Memory comes a-tied

CHORUS & OPHELIA: With bits and
rings and harsh temper
Through the columbines

OPHELIA: Before life

From life remembered
I'll take a little bite

CHORUS & OPHELIA: This time
all weeping ended
A scarlet bud in flight.

MINA appears.

MINA: What you warbling about?

OPHELIA: Don't know. Song come into
my head, best get it out, I said. Give it to
the moon.

MINA: Moon don't hear you.

OPHELIA: Might.

MINA: Moon's deaf. Always has been.
Don't you know anything?

OPHELIA: I'm ignorant.

MINA: That what Gertrude said? I
wouldn't listen to her. She's complex.

OPHELIA: How's that?

MINA: She's got a lot in her head. She's always scheming about something, fixing herself up. She's trying to make a name for herself.

OPHELIA: I thought she had one.

MINA: You're healing awful fast for a wounded one. You eat my scraps too, didn't you?

OPHELIA: Sugar pop. It's done now.

MINA: Get off your bum, I say. Get out. Go find comfort elsewhere. Who are you to come here with your story and get free everything? Food, clothes...

OPHELIA: Not new.

MINA: New enough. I've got old rag on. When do I get a new dress, eh? No singing to the moon for me. Got to work, don't I? H comes by, I got to serve him, do his pleasure. And what does he mean to me? Not lovey-dovey. Not a chance. He thinks one thing, I think another. He's got a bit of gold stashed, from what I hear. I could marry into that, if he'll have me. And he will. Don't you worry your pretty head. He will and I'll have everything and not have to suck on ring pop or sugar pop, but truffles, eh? Crème fraiche and strawberries. That'll be my daily serving. None of this chemical stuff, made up so you don't even know what it's made of, except it's sweet and cools the mouth from all. Rids the stink. In't that right? You listening to me?

OPHELIA: Of course.

MINA: You got a wandering mind. Strange one, you are. I could tell from when Gertrude brought you in. "Look at her," I said. "She's got stories up her sleeve, and won't she tell them, if she's pricked."

OPHELIA: What?

MINA: I stick you with a branch, you'd spill, wouldn't you?

OPHELIA: No stories to me. I'm clean. Fresh slate me.

MINA: Pure as snow?

OPHELIA: I am now.

MINA: You come from dirty water, you stay dirty. And ain't nothing wrong with that. Dirt's natural, part of life. Clean's what's unnatural. Only babies are born clean, and even then some…not a chance, right? I think pretending is wrong. That's all. Say what you are, be it, and you got a fair shot at life.

OPHELIA: I forget things. Slowly. Even drowning is in the past. Crushed daises in my hands

and long purple stems at my feet.
A picture only.
A portrait of another century
hanging on a wall in a museum.
That was me.
I point at the picture and smile,
pleased at my forgetting,
and a-comin back to where Jesus wept,
and He wept, didn't he?
That's another story,
but it's felt here on earth,
in this land, as we reach to heaven;
we feel weeping,
and sad tales of girls wronged
and left with broken families, and oh
how we weep, pitchers full, jars full,
wells of weeping,
but it don't mean anything.
Not to the girl. Not to the woman.
So, she returns, unmasks herself,
takes off the fresh flowered look
and replaces it with something true,
something real she can offer now,
cause she's cried and lost things,
she's an earned being;
and earning has value to the soul.

It makes a difference
now that she's on land
and walking
and not a-fearing herself anymore,
even if the rude boy is rude;
this she knows, she's lived it before,
and she's ready again.
Tell me what I don't know,
and I'll spin you a tale of woe
that will break your iron heart
and leave it on the floor.
Stick me with a hundred branches.
I'll heal.

MINA: That's most mouth I've heard
since you arrived.

OPHELIA: Is it?

MINA: I don't feel things quite that
way. But I think I know what you mean.
About weeping and that. Yeah. I've
done weeping a-plenty. Serves no one
but self, and self gets tired, don't she?

OPHELIA: Yes.

MINA: …You see to Gertrude?

OPHELIA: Now?

MINA: I've got to see H. We've an appointment.

OPHELIA: Who's H?

MINA: He's my man.

OPHELIA: The one with the gold?

MINA: If he'll have me.

OPHELIA: I'm not staying.

MINA: What?

OPHELIA: Gertrude said one night and I'm honoring that.

MINA: I don't mind. Company's nice. All the other girls leave. Gertrude's at the mirror all the time. I don't talk much to nobody except for H and he doesn't like talking.

OPHELIA: Mina.

MINA: Don't call my name.

OPHELIA: Mina.

MINA: I don't like it.

OPHELIA: It's a good name.

MINA: It's not mine. I took it from another girl. She died, right, having a baby? So, I changed my name for hers.

OPHELIA: What's your real name, then?

MINA: You won't tell?

OPHELIA: Who would I tell?

MINA: Rude one, Gertrude, R and G, they're a pair of sneaks…

OPHELIA: I won't tell.

MINA: …Lucinda.

OPHELIA: What?

MINA: That's my name.

OPHELIA: I like it.

MINA: Yeah? Doesn't sound funny?

OPHELIA: No, it's got music in it.

MINA: One day maybe…I'll change it back.

H is heard singing

"How should I know"

H : How should I know your true love know?
Shall I catch a jingle jangle?

MINA: That's him.

H sings.

H: Shall I take you down and drop your crown?
Shall I wear a spingle spangle?

OPHELIA: Off, then, Lucinda.

MINA: Yeah.

OPHELIA: And get paid.

H is seen. He sings to Mina.

H : How should I know
your true love know?
Shall I catch a jingle jangle?
Shall I take you down
and drop your crown?
Shall I wear a spingle spangle?

Gertrude appears.

How should I know

your true love know?

H kisses Mina. They walk away.

GERTRUDE: *(to herself)* What's true here?

OPHELIA: What?

GERTRUDE: You're better?

OPHELIA: I'm rested. Mina's gone out.

GERTRUDE: As well as she should. Was it H?

OPHELIA: Yes.

GERTRUDE: He made me a gift not too long ago. A pearl necklace. He likes Mina well enough.

OPHELIA: Likes you?

GERTRUDE: I'm well liked. What of it?

OPHELIA: Nothing. You should wear them, the pearls.

GERTRUDE
No need. If some function come up

[Gertrude rings for tea. R and G appear tea for Gertrude and Ophelia. They stand at attention.]

OPHELIA: A social thing?

GERTRUDE: Society is important, being well regarded... Society is what holds civilization together.

OPHELIA: Never thought that way.

GERTRUDE: Such is your fate.

OPHELIA: How's that?

GERTRUDE: How you think, fit into society, and be part of things, determines your course in life.

OPHELIA: I think opposite.

GERTRUDE: Do you now?

OPHELIA: I think the more you fit in, the more left out you are.

GERTRUDE: Makes no sense to me.

OPHELIA: You fit in to other people's needs, you are left out, do you see?

GERTRUDE: Individuality?

OPHELIA: Yeah.

GERTRUDE: It's a stupid word. One of your book words, isn't it? Won't find that word in a magazine.

OPHELIA: You like society?

GERTRUDE: I like wearing nice things, being seen. I don't pretend I'm liked. That's of no concern. Mina's the one who's got to watch. She's falling for H.

Got all sorts of illusions, that girl. He'll never have her, not as a wife.

OPHELIA: Why not?

GERTRUDE: He won't marry. Not interested.

OPHELIA: I don't understand.

GERTRUDE: He's that kind of man. Won't ever marry.

OPHELIA: You should tell her.

GERTRUDE: Mina? No. Let her earn her keep, dream a bit. It'll all come crashing soon enough. Always does.

Gertrude indicates she has finished her tea. R and G retrieve teacups and saucers from Ophelia and Gertrude, and they exit.

You're putting in for the night?

OPHELIA: Not yet.

GERTRUDE: You're not much use if you don't get your beauty sleep.

OPHELIA: I'll be in a bit. There are too many stars out.

GERTRUDE: Dead particles. Isn't that what they are?

OPHELIA: They're past and future life.

GERTRUDE: Well, that's novel.

Gertrude exits. Ophelia sings.

"Be fallen" (reprise)

OPHELIA: Fall and be fallen
All around is sky
Deep eternal winter
For a muted sigh.

She is joined by Chorus of Ophelias. They repeat the song now in a roundelay. Ophelia and the chorus are entranced by their own

*desires. An erotic gavotte – a movement
sequence - ensues wherein dreams of
pleasure and violence are intimated.
Gertrude, Mina, H, R and G may take part
in this dance-dream. After a short while, the
roundelay ends as Rude Boy appears, and
the chorus (and others) fades. The Rude Boy
is bruised.*

RUDE BOY: Had to see you all right,
couldn't think, got in fight, not fair what
you've done, I believe in fairness, in
what's right.

OPHELIA: What are you doing here?

RUDE BOY: Don't care what. She can
throw me out. I know her. Gertrude.
She's got a waspish tongue. Toss me
down river.

OPHELIA: Hush.

RUDE BOY: Why? What you going to
do, cold one?

OPHELIA: What do you mean?

RUDE BOY: Not a note, not a call or holler. What we done, what that meant? Fool's game?

OPHELIA: I thought we were alike.

RUDE BOY: Thought wrong. My head's turnt. I'm starting to think of things I haven't thought in a while. Don't like that. My life's just fine. On a road, that's me, on a path I understand.

OPHELIA: You don't love me.

RUDE BOY: How'd you know?

OPHELIA: You left me, didn't you? Didn't care what happened.

RUDE BOY: I leave everyone. That's just me, what I do.

OPHELIA: You won't let me hold onto a name.

RUDE BOY: Aren't you going to kiss me? I've been hit.

OPHELIA: You were in a fight.

RUDE BOY: Yeah I was, and wasn't meant to be.

OPHELIA: Are you blaming me?

RUDE BOY: I need to see you, all right.

OPHELIA: I'm right here.

RUDE BOY: No kind words?

OPHELIA: What do you want me to say?

RUDE BOY: Sweet things, tender in my ear so I can dream at night and fall asleep. I have trouble sleeping.

OPHELIA: Look for someone else.

RUDE BOY: What'd you mean?

OPHELIA: I'm not good. I told you that. You've mistaken me.

RUDE BOY: You've a good heart. I know that.

OPHELIA: And you cut me open while I was sleeping.

RUDE BOY: Wasn't me.

OPHELIA: Tell me another lie.

RUDE BOY: I've never done anything of the kind.

OPHELIA: Be honest. That's all we can be to each other.

RUDE BOY: I need a kiss.

OPHELIA: No.

RUDE BOY: Spite me; be cruel.

OPHELIA: As you were to me, so I will be.

RUDE BOY: Call me Hamlet.

OPHELIA: Don't.

RUDE BOY: He was yours, wasn't he? You still love him.

OPHELIA: I don't love anyone.

RUDE BOY: What were his words like?

OPHELIA: You know what they were.

RUDE BOY: "You nickname God's creatures and make wantonness your ignorance."

OPHELIA: Just so.

RUDE BOY: "What should such fellows as I do crawling between earth and heaven?"

OPHELIA: Make me believe.

RUDE BOY: I did love you.

OPHELIA: Once.

RUDE BOY: I do love you.

OPHELIA: I will not be deceived.

RUDE BOY: What deceit is this? What deceit do you see?

OPHELIA: You lie to me.

RUDE BOY: I am honest.

OPHELIA: And fair. Yes. And what of it?

RUDE BOY: "Could beauty have better commerce than with honesty?"

OPHELIA: You mock me.

RUDE BOY: Look at me.

OPHELIA: No.

RUDE BOY: Make me mad. Come on. Strip me of reason. I have no need of it anymore.

OPHELIA: Do not say such things.

RUDE BOY: Such things as I desire and more. Strip me, cruel and merciless heart. Rob every part of me. Use me for sport. Give me a start.

OPHELIA: And what will you give me?

RUDE BOY: Everything.

OPHELIA: Be honest.

RUDE BOY: Kiss take hand now, all right; I am rude, I always said I was, but not meant harm, not for nothing. Ain't deserve this. Be my wanton mistress, and I'll be your wretch.

OPHELIA: …One kiss.

RUDE BOY: Yeah.

OPHELIA: And then you go.

RUDE BOY: I'm not in a book. I don't act on command.

OPHELIA: You ask too much.

RUDE BOY: I ask for nothing, only what's deserved.

OPHELIA: …What is love if not what tears you?

RUDE BOY: I don't know what you mean.

OPHELIA: Take and be true.

She kisses him. They make love.

Eight

R and G overlook…

R: Seen her kind.

G: Before and after.

R: And after that.

G: The ones who tell and refuse to be told.

R: The crushed ones who come back.

G: Seeking to mend? Wrong place.

R: Wrong time.

G: No mending here. This is a split place, water's crooked, trees grow wrong side up. She should know.

R: She's not thinking.

G: Thinking too much, I think. Thinking plenty what shouldn't. And what should…

Beat.

G: Thinks nothing of us.

R: Not a thank you.

G: She's a-cursed.

R: Singing to the moon. Odder and odder still.

G: We sung once.

R: Good form.

G: We had, didn't we? Love songs hundreds of years old.

R: Ballads.

G: We knew them all. What was - ?

R sings:

"Lonesome Child"

R: Lonesome child, done run away

G sings next line of the song.

G: Hold back tears another day.

*They sing, slowly remembering the tune
they used to sing long ago.*

R: Birds of sorrow,
where have you gone?

G: Over valley to catch the sun.

R: Lonesome child, done run away.

G: Blooms of laurel upon her grave.

R: Take my words as sweet advice.

G: There's no love without a price.

Confident now of the tune and of their
memory, R sings, followed by G.

R: Lonesome child, be not a-feared
Love will last a hundred years
Field of promise, where are you now?
Take this daughter upon your brow.

G: Lonesome child, be not a-feared
Lift your voices for all to hear
Take this song on blessed wing
Silent falls first kiss of spring.

They dance joyfully. And then they sing.

R & G: Lonesome child, done run away.
Blooms of laurel upon her grave
Take my words as sweet advice.
There's no love without a price.

Ophelia and Rude Boy's love-making
becomes more savage. Ophelia leaves Rude
Boy. The chorus of Ophelias wakes.

Nine

Ophelia at dawn. The Chorus of Ophelias is heard softly. Gertrude and R , may act as the Chorus (as indicated).

OPHELIA: *(To Rude Boy in mind)* I tear what I most want from me; it is what I've learned. And what's torn remains. In this book I write in my head the words cling to your frame; I have learnt every part of you, and accepted your madness, nothing is what cannot be and what it seems… so be it. I am in your debt. Seek me out. On this morn that chills the warm spine. Come to my bed. Make of me a whore. Honor what you've said.

The Chorus breathes.

The ghost child inside me rises up from under a mossy ground, from water buried.
The child makes noise. I listen to it.

Ophelia's Double rises up out of the chorus, which surrounds Ophelia. This role should be played by the actor playing G.

OPHELIA'S DOUBLE: Fiery glass and a cold tongue wreck the man spoken for and to be spoken of.

OPHELIA: What's this, she cries? Who is she?

OPHELIA'S DOUBLE: Who are the girls that cry at break of morning with violets in their hair:
"Bonny sweet and will he not come again?"

OPHELIA: Will he not come again to mourn for me, to surrender his will? Is there no vengeance I can seek or peace to be made at the end of this day?

OPHELIA'S DOUBLE: At the end of this day, bonny sweet man of rude inclination will

OPHELIA & CHORUS: Shh.

OPHELIA'S DOUBLE: He will beg for forgiveness or toss your soul down into the well sealed with another girl's breath, another girl's...

OPHELIA & CHORUS: Shh.

OPHELIA: Speak reason, child.

OPHELIA'S DOUBLE: It is hard to speak when one has lived underwater for so long. My throat is swollen and salt burdened.

OPHELIA: I must think.

OPHELIA'S DOUBLE: You must grow old and be a full woman and forget everything. The rude boy will find another and another will be claimed, and your remembrance will be ever fresh. Ophelia, is that your name?

OPHELIA: Yes.

OPHELIA'S DOUBLE: It is my name, too. Hear it?

CHORUS: [sings slowly, under] "Ophelia, find her a way...."

OPHELIA: It echoes.

OPHELIA'S DOUBLE: The O lingers like a refrain from a ballad sung by women spent over years of breaking.

OPHELIA: Bonny sweet and hold on to me a little longer.

OPHELIA'S DOUBLE: And in holding what reward will you give me for my constancy?

OPHELIA: I have been daughter,

OPHELIA'S DOUBLE: sister, mother and your other self regained. I have watched you and have kept watching

and have waited many a day for you to
release me, and release yourself from all
breaking

CHORUS & OPHELIA'S DOUBLE:
sighing

OPHELIA'S DOUBLE: In water still,
in drips and tears, I burrow. I carve.
I ravage unborn and unwanted,
reborn now as your mirror.
What say you, Ophelia?
What say I, in pity's name,
 in loose shame, and brazen lunacy?
Hold on a little longer,
but how shall I be paid?
…confused and aching,
become unbewildered
I am your other glass, Ophelia.
Remember me.

OPHELIA: What?

OPHELIA'S DOUBLE: On the morn
suddenly very brave the same song in a
different larynx.

CHORUS & OPHELIA'S DOUBLE:
Remember…

The Chorus fades as Mina appears, singing.

"Mina's song"

MINA: I was now
I was seen
All through rock and stream
Hey
Call the fine young dandies

Would you would be?
Would you with me?
All through birch and sea
Hey
Call the fine young ladies

Pity, dear
That you see
How I came to be so free?
This is the legacy
Of the water's mercy.

Here, dear
In this stream
Hold
The fiery being
Hey
Don't look now.

Time Shift.

MINA
Remember me?

OPHELIA: What?

MINA: H asked me to marry him last night. Where you been?

OPHELIA: Here.

MINA: Weren't. Came looking for you. You were gone. Have you got blood on you?

OPHELIA: What?

MINA: You're not of right mind.
Where's the Rude Boy? He leave you
again?

OPHELIA: I don't remember.

MINA: Think nothing of it. One thing
Gertrude taught me is to not want
another as if life…
Crave and satisfy but not to your end.

OPHELIA: I heard my child speaking.

MINA: You've child?

OPHELIA: I think it was inside me.

MINA: An unborn thing?

OPHELIA: Yes.

MINA: I've had that. Got rid of it. Heard
nothing.

OPHELIA: Not even speaking?

MINA: Put it away, out of my head.

OPHELIA: How'd you do that?

MINA: Teach myself breathing.

OPHELIA: Special like?

MINA: Like a swallow. A bird. Tiny breaths every time a thought comes. And it's gone.

OPHELIA: Teach me.

MINA: Now?

OPHELIA: Yes.

MINA: Now, they're tiny, right? Like you don't even know you're doing them. Think you're a bird. A little beak, little mouth, begging at mama bird's feet. Yeah. That's right. And the tiniest breath… and another… and all the unborn will fade….

Mina breathes.
Ophelia breathes.
Shallow breaths.
Tiny breaths escape from mouths of the
Chorus.
They build.

Ten

H sings.

"Fade fast"

H: Fade fast
On love askance
What sorrow brings
To waking eye

A beating rain
Cleans the wound
Leaves the lover
No place to hide.

Hurry now,
Wanton girl
Lift your eyes
To the widening, widening sky.

Rude Boy appears and joins H in song,
taking the lead.

RUDE BOY & H: Hurry now,

wanton girl
Lift your eyes
To the widening, widening sky.

RUDE BOY: Where will you go
now that you're losing?
A lover's laugh
is your only sign.

RUDE BOY & H: Hurry now,
wanton child
let your eyes
brim with sweet, sweet delight.

Hurry now,
wanton girl
Lift your eyes
To the widening, widening sky.

Rude Boy lets loose in the duet:

Hurry now
Wanton child
Lift your eyes
To the widening, widening sky

RUDE BOY: I'll send a note
In your restless ear.
"Waste tomorrow.
Keep love in light."

*Song ends as Rude Boy drowns in woe with
H.*

RUDE BOY: Like she didn't even want
me.

H: Cut you?

RUDE BOY: Dug her nails in. Right on
my skin.

H: You're not made for love.

RUDE BOY: That's not love. That's
creepy.

H: Ain't it?

RUDE BOY: ...What?

H: I got Mina full time.

RUDE BOY: You?

H: True as my word.

RUDE BOY: How'd you swing that?

H: Asked her. Simple. No complications in my life.

RUDE BOY: I need to see Ophelia again.

H: You won't quit, will you?

RUDE BOY: We got a wrong start. That's clear to me. We shouldn't have met like we did. It was too quick.

H: She's with child.

RUDE BOY: Who said that?

H: Rumor has it.

RUDE BOY: Since when do you -?

H: I don't, but could be true. What? You don't think…?

RUDE BOY: Don't know.

H: You don't want, then?

RUDE BOY: I have to see her.

H: Your head IS turnt.

RUDE BOY: I need to.

H: Begin again?

RUDE BOY: Yes.

H: Fool's errand.

RUDE BOY: It's not.

H: You're not thinking straight.

RUDE BOY: What'd you mean?

H: Who are you beholden to?

RUDE BOY: Eh?

H: Think about it.

RUDE BOY: …Where I come from, I suppose.

H: Inheritance. Not love. That's what ties you.

RUDE BOY: I wish we were in school again.

H: No responsibility?

RUDE BOY: Clear lines. World not messing about with you. No madness undoing what you've built.

H: School's gone.

RUDE BOY: In the wild unbroken scheme of things, what's left us? A chase for something passionate, remarkable, strange that we can't control. That's what I seek, have sought, need. Is it wrong?

H: If you don't mind someone's nails on your skin.

RUDE BOY: Hit me.

H: What?

RUDE BOY: You start the fight this time. I want to know what it feels like to lose everything.

H: With an open fist?

RUDE BOY: With what you'll give me.

H strikes Rude Boy again and again and again. Rude Boy does not fight back. H continues striking him until he cannot any longer.

Eleven

Gertrude stands in the field. She watches Ophelia leave. She speak-sings in a voice unleashed from her past.

"Gertrude's Lament"

GERTUDE: Through wet fields
she walks
With the ghost of a child on her back
Ophelia is leaving.
Ophelia is leaving.

Breath on breath
she takes each step
As if she were breaking
As if she were breaking.

Tell the child I won't wait
Or cry for her return
She passes through, passes through
my shaken memory

Breath on breath

she takes each step
As if she were breaking

Ophelia is the daughter left
The other side of my vanity.

Twelve

Ophelia on the road.

OPHELIA: Breath, breath, breath

Rude Boy appears.

RUDE BOY: Forgive me.

OPHELIA: What brings you?

RUDE BOY: Folly.

OPHELIA: That's right. Don't want you anymore.

RUDE BOY: Let me recognize myself.

OPHELIA: In me? That's self-serving, if ever I may say.

RUDE BOY: Begin again.

OPHELIA: What for?

RUDE BOY: I think if we....

OPHELIA: There's no beginning.
There's just end. See? Easy that way.

RUDE BOY: If you've a child, I want...

OPHELIA: Did you get into another
fight? You're more bruised than before.

RUDE BOY: It was my punishment.

OPHELIA: There's no child. She's gone.
In watery vapor now.

RUDE BOY: And you're to drown
again?

OPHELIA: No. What made you think
that?

RUDE BOY: Heading toward water.

OPHELIA: Heading somewhere else. If I wanted to live the rest of my life as a whore, I would, but don't want and don't want eternal wanting either. That's a fool way to live under water or not. Don't need you. To curse me and damn me all the time, and I'm always the lesser? Ain't for me. World's too big.

RUDE BOY: World's too small.

OPHELIA: Don't follow me.

RUDE BOY: ...Ophelia.

OPHELIA: What?

RUDE BOY: I'd rather be buried with you than not see you again.

OPHELIA: Full of words, aren't you? When I don't need them.

RUDE BOY: ...I'll be Hamlet.

OPHELIA: And we'll what? Go mad together?

RUDE BOY: Whatever you wish.

OPHELIA: …You've come to the wrong place for mercy.

Beat.

RUDE BOY: If you could have anything…

OPHELIA: A new memory.

RUDE BOY: That's what you'd like?

OPHELIA: More than love. Yes.
I was my mother's child.
And my father's child.
And my brother's, too.
And when they were dead,
I was my lover's child,
and he hurt me true. This is my riddle,
what I carry inside me. Un-riddle me
from this. And give me another life.

RUDE BOY: I was my father's child and he haunted me, and I lived my life inside his haunting. So, I turned myself into something unknown, hollow, hostile, and worn. This was my other life, which I need leave.

OPHELIA: And you leave and you find

RUDE BOY: …A woman standing on the road heading toward something

OPHELIA: Not wanting.

RUDE BOY: Not dreaming

OPHELIA: Not remembering her child's cry.

Pause. Rude Boy takes little bird breaths as Ophelia once did.

RUDE BOY: Breath, breath, breath.

OPHELIA: You hear her breathing.

RUDE BOY: This is the breath to go on living

OPHELIA: And it isn't even

RUDE BOY: Barely heard

OPHELIA: A tiny thing

RUDE BOY: That will hold her through eternity.

In the distance, the chorus of Ophelias is heard: audible breaths.

Look at me now.

OPHELIA: Hamlet in tatters

RUDE BOY: Un-masked, unadorned.

OPHELIA: A rude boy. That's all.

RUDE BOY: That's all I ever was.

OPHELIA: And for this such…

RUDE BOY: Don't say it.
I am nothing more than what you see.

OPHELIA: One last kiss, and then no more

RUDE BOY: Because soon?

OPHELIA: Soon, soon, soon you'll have none of me.

They kiss.
Ophelia gently breaks away from him, and walks away.
She is on the road; she walks for miles.
She releases her clothes and leaves all remnant of her past behind,
as Rude Boy watches her, unable to move.

Thirteen

R and G look at the water.

R: Left how she came. Quick.

G: Heard say he followed her.

R: The rude boy?

G: Tales are told.

R: She'll have none of him.

G: Love lingers.

R: What do you know?

G: I've loved.

R: Have you?

G: Think I haven't?

Beat.

R: Look at the water. It's rippling.

G: Undercurrent. Something caught.

R: ...I'd like a swim.

G: Now?

R: I haven't swum in years. Take my clothes off and dip in.

G: You'd do that?

R: Wouldn't you?

G: I could.

Beat.

R: She came up out of the water and forgot herself.

G: And gained her reason.

R: What's to become of her?

G: What's to become of any of us?

R: Sorry creatures.

G: Looking to be undone.

R and G jump into the water, and swim.
They swim joyously,
and disappear under the water's surface.
Ophelia continues walking.

Optional Song:
a hidden track for *12 Ophelias*

These lyrics may be set to serve as pre-show or prelude to the piece, or may be sung as a post-show coda after the end of the play.

"To see what I'm seeing,
you have to look"

in waking darkness
long ago
when earth was red
unsettled in desire
lightning struck was I

on diamond path
burning low
when sky was held
unmoored in heart's fire
shadow struck was I

night spent
in accusing sorrow

I waited for you, I waited for you
ancient truth
a selfish desire
to see what i'm seeing, you have to look.

and so I was
claimed in memory
shadow struck
the first time

and as you go
the world finds me
broken in light.

Caridad Svich is a playwright-songwriter-translator and editor of Cuban-Spanish-Argentine-Croatian descent. Key works include *Alchemy of Desire/Dead-Man's Blues, Fugitive Pieces, The Booth Variations, Iphigenia Crash Land Falls on the Neon Shell That Was Once Her Heart (a rave fable),* and *The Labyrinth of Desire.* She has translated nearly all of Federico Garcia Lorca's plays and works by Calderon de la Barca, Lope de Vega, Antonio Buero Vallejo and contemporary works by dramatists from Mexico and Cuba. She is editor of several books on theatre & performance published by Manchester University Press/UK, TCG and Smith & Kraus. She is alumna playwright of New Dramatists, contributing editor of *TheatreForum,* associate editor of *Contemporary Theatre Review* (Routledge/UK), affiliate artist of New Georges, and founder of NoPassport. She holds an MFA from UCSD. Her website is www.caridadsvich.com

NoPassport

No Passport is a Pan-American theatre alliance & press devoted to live, virtual and print action, advocacy, and change toward the fostering of cross-cultural diversity in the arts with an emphasis on the embrace of the hemispheric spirit in US Latina/o and Latin-American theatremaking.

NoPassport Press' Theatre & Performance PlayTexts Series and its Dreaming the Americas Series promotes new writing for the stage, texts on theory and practice, and theatrical translations.

Series Editors:
Jorge Huerta, Otis Ramsey Zoe, Caridad Svich

Advisory Board:
Daniel Banks, Amparo Garcia-Crow, Maria M. Delgado, Randy Gener, Elana Greenfield, Christina Marin, Antonio Ocampo-Guzman, Sarah Cameron Sunde, Saviana Stanescu, Tamara Underiner, Patricia Ybarra

This text is set in Palatino Linotype 12 and 14.

Lightning Source UK Ltd.
Milton Keynes UK
UKOW051201180512

192841UK00001B/10/P